GEORGIA PEACH

EMMA BRAY

Gage

I'M PISSED AS HELL. Here I am sitting in a black SUV in one of the wealthiest neighborhoods in Atlanta doing recon on this entitled motherfucker who thinks he's going to get one over on the notorious Gage Morelli.

Not today, asshat.

I suppose I could have sent one of my goons to rough him up, but this debt is more personal. It's not about the money he owes me so much as it is the respect.

It's the lack of respect that really gets to me. This

guys *knows* the kingpin that I am. He knows I rule all of New York with an iron-clad fist. Yet, he thinks he can borrow what he needs to get his business off the ground and then stiff me?

I sneer at the pristine white mansion sprawled across the street from where my black SUV sits inconspicuously. It has thick fucking columns lining the huge front porch in true old-world Southern colonial-style fashion.

This fucker doesn't come from old-world money, though. That's for sure. He might want to paint a pretty picture of being the perfect southern gentleman, but I know better. I know the kind of sick shit this fuck's into.

He thinks I don't know he lied to me about what he needed the money for. It was only after I loaned him the millions that I found out what his warehousing business is truly a front for—an industry that makes even a man like me sick.

My blood boils at just the thought of it as my eyes rake over every inch of his property I can see from my vantage point here in the shadows. I bet he thought he was safe from me in his ostentatious home in Atlanta.

He thought wrong.

There's no end to my reach. My headquarters might be in New York, but there's not a place in this whole goddamn world—let alone the nation—where he can hide from me.

He's ignored my warnings and put me off for the last time. He's living under some misguided notion that I won't kill him because I won't get my money if I do that.

He underestimates me. Not only do I not *really* need the money, but I will fucking kill him, and I *will* still get what's owed me too.

But first, I know exactly how to strike the fear of god in him.

His daughter.

Gage

Jesus Christ. I never expected her to be so beautiful. I waited all day for Sinclair's daughter to come rolling in in the little red Mercedes her daddy bought her.

She steps out of the car now, and the first thing I see are long, smooth legs that seem to go on forever. She gracefully exits the car like a model, still wearing a pair of fashionably oversized sunglasses. She's not tall by any means—maybe five-foot-five at the most, but she's a leggy thing with toned calves, shapely thighs, and an ass as ripe-looking as a sweet Georgia peach.

She's wearing some sort of floral-print dress that comes down mid-thigh, but instead of wearing high heels like most of the women I'm accustomed to, she has on a simple pair of leather sandals.

Her honey-colored hair falls down her back in a flash of silk, and I watch as the summer breeze catches it and swirls it out all around her. She pushes her sunglasses to the top of her head to hold her hair back from her a face, using them as a makeshift headband.

I zoom in on her face with the camera I'm holding up and snap several photos. When I'm confronted with the lushest pair of sinfully puffy pink lips I've ever seen, I'm suddenly very glad I didn't outsource this particular job to one of my men.

I don't want anyone else stalking her this way, spying on her like this.

Her eyes are a chocolate brown framed by thick, dark lashes. They're big and soft and innocent-looking, and I feel something tighten within my chest as I look in them.

She walks over to one of the peach trees in the yard and reaches up, plucking one off of the low-hanging branches. The whisper of a smile plays on her lips as she lifts the fruit up to her mouth and takes a bite.

Juice flows from the corners of her mouth. She holds up a hand to catch it from dribbling down her little chin and closes her eyes as she tips her head back and savors the sweetness of the ripe fruit, her lips wet and glistening.

I feel my cock surging to full mast in my slacks.

Fuuuck.

She has no idea what she's doing. To her, she's just enjoying a peach, but the filthy, sexual images the sight conjures up in my mind are enough to make a lesser man cream in his pants.

She looks too sweet. Too innocent. Angelic.

And the thoughts I'm having about her right now are far from any of those things. They're downright criminal.

I shake my head and try to focus. Her beauty changes nothing. Her father fucked up, and in this game, she's unfortunately just a pawn to get her old man to fall into line.

She doesn't deserve this. It's not her fault. She can't help being the daughter of my enemy.

But it is what is.

And the devil is coming for her.

CHAPTER ONE

Ava

I CAN'T SHAKE IT. I've had this strange feeling for the past few days. Little prickles on the back of my neck. A weird sensation that makes the tiny hairs on my arms stand up.

I keep looking over my shoulder like I'm being watched, but nothing is ever there.

Paranoid much, Ava? I ask myself with a roll of my eyes. I've obviously watched one too many of those true crime documentaries. It probably doesn't help that I watch them right before I fall asleep. That stuff is probably implanting itself deep in my subconscious or something, and that's why I'm freaking out right now.

I finish tying my flower crown together. I crafted it from the pink and white hydrangeas that flank the pool behind Daddy's mansion. I'd quickly nabbed a couple of blooms when the gardener wasn't looking before I took off into the wheat fields that line the back of our property. My father isn't exactly a farmer, but he owns plenty of property, and he grows wheat and other crops on it. He's more like an agricultural investor, I guess.

Whatever he does keeps him pretty busy, though. I know he just bought some new buildings, and he's been gone more than usual.

I sigh and plop my flower crown on my head. I realize it's childish to still make them and put them on my head—especially now that I'm officially an adult at eighteen—but I've been doing it ever since I was a little girl. Call it my ritual or whatever, but when I need to think or clear my head, I grab some flowers from the garden, dash out here to the wheat field, twist the flowers into a crown, and then smash them onto my head before laying in the tall wheat and staring up at the clouds as I get lost in my thoughts.

Today my thoughts are on college. I'm set to start

at Emory University in just a couple of months, and Daddy has already been onto me about picking a major.

I'm still no closer to choosing than I was in high school.

It's not that nothing interests me. On the contrary, it's that *so* much interests me. How am I supposed to choose one thing to do for the rest of my life?

Of course, Daddy is pushing me to be a lawyer, but I already know he wants me to work where the money's at—in criminal defense. But I just don't know how I'd feel about defending people who might actually be guilty of heinous crimes. Everybody knows there's no money in prosecution, but I think I'd want to be on the right side of the law if I was going to do it. I don't know how I'd feel if I got someone off who was accused of doing something horrible like raping a woman—especially if come to find out they really did it.

So I'm pretty sure being a lawyer is out.

I'm not sure my heart lies in medicine either. I can devour all the latest scientific journals, but the thought of cutting into skin or dealing with blood just makes me shiver.

So there goes doctor or veterinarian.

I hold my hands up over my face and groan. Why is it so hard for me to pick something? I envy my fellow classmates who've known what they wanted to be since they were nine. Seriously, I know some people who've wanted to be teachers or doctors or lawyers or firefighters since they were little kids and are already well on their way to making those dreams become their reality.

Why is it so hard for me?

I frown. Maybe it's because I've always kept my head in the clouds and daydreamed. I love nothing more than getting lost in a good book and spent countless hours out here in this very field playing with imaginary friends when I was a little girl. As an only child, I had to develop a vivid imagination. I held fairy court out here where I was the fairy queen with my flower crown.

I sigh again and tell myself that I've still got plenty of time to choose a major. The first two years of college are mostly just core classes anyway. Surely by the time I become a college junior, I'll have grown up enough to figure out what I want to do with the rest of my life.

I stare up at the clouds moving slowly overhead in the robin's egg blue sky and let the stress of adult choices release from my mind. One of the clouds looks like a crab, and it makes me think of the time when my mother was still alive and she and Daddy took me to the Gulf in Alabama. I'd seen a live crab skittering along the beach, and it had struck me as odd that it wasn't red like Sebastian from *The Little Mermaid* but a pale white color, almost blending in with the sand.

From there, my mind wanders onto how cool it would be to have an exciting life like a Disney princess. Ariel had always been my favorite princess, closely followed by Belle. Why couldn't life be an adventure like in children's movies or like in the books I read?

Maybe I'll write books or the screenplays for children's movies. That's a job I can see myself doing for the rest of my life, but I can only imagine the disappointment on Daddy's face if I tell him I'm going to a top university for an English Lit degree rather than something big like medicine or law.

I yawn as the warm sun kisses my skin, covering me like a blanket. My limbs get heavier, and I close my eyes, floating in that hazy half awake, half asleep state of doziness.

I don't know how long I lay there in limbo between the real world and dreamland, but when I do finally flutter my eyes open, my heart jumps up into my chest with a gasp.

Ice. The iciest, bluest eyes I've ever seen are gazing down at me, piercing me with their intensity.

Dark hair, hair as dark as night falls onto a strong, hard forehead, a masculine forehead.

Strong jawlines taper down until my eyes are drawn to lips that are conversely lush against the hard planes of the man's face.

He looks like an angel—a dark angel, that is.

My heart beat ticks up—in fear or excitement or a mixture of both I'm not sure.

I open my mouth—to ask who he is or scream, I'm not sure which—but in the next moment his hand comes down to silence me with a sickly sweet-smelling cloth, and I plummet into blackness.

⁂

Ava

When I come to, I'm laying on something plush and soft. I start to sink back down into the luxuriousness, but my head thrums with a persistent ache, and I know that something's not right. This doesn't feel like my bed at home, and then I sit up with a bolt as I suddenly remember what happened.

Piercing blue eyes. A darkly handsome man. A cloth coming down over my nose, drugging me.

The world spins as I sit up too quickly. I raise a hand to my head to steady myself. My head feels so heavy.

"Careful, princess," a deep voice says. It comes from the corner of the room, and my eyes dart frantically that way, seeking the source of the voice.

Although it's dark in the room and the figure sits in the shadows, those same icy blue eyes spear me, shining in the darkness like blue flames.

Fear churns to the surface as I realize this stranger has abducted me. Who is he? What does he want with me?

A quick glance around the shadowed room reveals that I'm in a rather swanky place—not the types of basements and warehouses kidnapping victims usually seem to find themselves in. On the contrary, I've been laid out on a plush four-poster bed with thick blankets. I glance down over my frame and realize with relief that my clothes are still on, so it doesn't seem like I've been violated in *that* type of way—not yet anyway.

I look back up and see those twin flames still trained intently on me. "No, princess. I didn't rape you."

His voice almost sounds angry, like he's offended that I would even think that he would do something like that, but what am I supposed to think? I don't know this guy at all, and he *did* steal me right out of my own backyard.

"Who are you? What do you want with me?" I almost cringe at myself. I sound like the stereotypical kidnapping victim from all those Lifetime movies I've watched. But really what else could be said in a situation like this?

He reaches over to flick on the lamp sitting on the table next to where he sits in his chair like it's a throne, like he's some sort of king—king of the darkness. The room illuminates in a soft glow, and I can better make out my surroundings.

The room is masculine and contemporary. It's high-end, and I can't help thinking if this guy has money like this, why does he feel the need to kidnap girls?

My eyes fully take in his tall form. He's wearing a suit like he's a businessman or something. He's sinfully handsome in that dangerous, bad boy sort of way. Surely he could have any woman he wants.

So why me? Why has he taken me? It makes no sense.

Unless maybe this is *how* he makes his money, by kidnapping girls and holding them for ransom.

"Whatever you're wanting, my father will pay..." I offer.

His lips tip up into a cold smile as he leans forward, draping his arms on his knees. "Oh, that's what I'm counting on, princess."

My heart does this weird flutter-plummet within my chest. I'm both relieved and disappointed by his response. If all he wants is money, daddy has plenty of it, and I know he'll pay any ransom to get me back. I'm his only child, after all.

I'm happy because this means I should be on my way home in no time, right? So, why do I feel a prickle of disappointment and self-loathing that the only reason this man took me was for the money he could get for a ransom? I mean, I should be glad he doesn't want me in a sexual way because that means he won't rape me.

But of course why would a guy who looks like him want me anyway? He looks to be in his early thirties. Everything about him screams man, worldly, and sophisticated. What would he want with a silly little girl like me? I blush when I remember how he'd found me with a flower crown on my head like a baby. How long had he been watching me?

I give my head a tiny shake to try to clear my mind. These crazy thoughts must just be after effects of whatever he drugged me with. Chloroform if I had to guess. In any case, just because he's the most attractive man I've ever seen doesn't mean that he's not dangerous. I should be thrilled he's not attracted to me and pray that he doesn't want to do worse things to me.

"Right," I nod at him like we're conducting a business meeting, "so if you just let me contact him and tell him how much you want, I'm sure he'll get it to you as soon as possible and you can let me go."

He leans back in the chair again, hooking a foot over his knee and stroking his thumb over his lower lip as he regards me thoughtfully.

"Tell me, Ava," he says slowly, drawing out the syllables of my name in a way that makes a tingle run up my spine, "Do I look like a man who needs money to you?"

I stare at him before swallowing and shaking my head.

He shakes his head along with me. "This is about so much more than money, my little Georgia peach."

"What's it about then?" my voice is barely more than a whisper.

He frowns before answering, "Nothing that you need to worry your pretty little head about."

Silence lingers between us for a moment. When

it's obvious he's not going to say anything more, I make myself ask the question that's burning inside my brain.

"Are you going to hurt me?"

<hr>

Gage

Are you going to hurt me?

Those words from her sweet lips are almost my undoing. They slam into me, reminding me again of how innocent this girl is in all of this. After watching her for weeks and using every resource I have available to me to find out everything I could about her, I'm convinced she has no idea about her father's extracurricular activities.

She's just a pawn in a game her father's trying to play with me.

And I don't know why, but I hate myself for using her like this.

It's never bothered me before to use someone as a pawn to conduct business. Of course, I've never kidnapped anyone before either—much less the most beautiful angel I've ever seen.

She looks so much like a little lady, but she's also so much like a child. She was wearing a flower crown on her head when I abducted her, for Chrissakes. I'd watched in fascination as she'd sat in that fucking wheat field and braided the fucking thing.

I see her watching me warily from where she still sits on the bed. She's made no move to rise other than to sit up. No screaming fits. No running from me in a panic. She's pretty much kept her head about her, and that actually impresses me.

"I promise you no harm will come to you when you're in my care," I vow to her. I've never meant anything more.

I know it's probably not my best move. I should probably tell her no harm will come to her so long as she does what I say or some typical kidnapper shit like that, but the truth slips out instead. I mean what I said. I'd cut off my hand before I let any harm come to her. The irony that I've probably already emotionally traumatized her by kidnapping her isn't lost on me. But I sure as hell won't let any physical harm come to her, and I'm going to try my best to make sure that she's not emotionally scarred either when all this is over with.

See, something happened during my weeks of watching her.

I became somehow mesmerized by her. She captivated me the moment I first saw her, and as I continued to gather intel about her, I came to look forward to every moment of the day that I stalked her. By watching her, I feel like I got to know her.

I know that her favorite drink at Starbucks is some sugary sweet crap called a caramel macchiato. I know that she's popular on the surface in the city of Atlanta and that she has tons of "friends," but she's not particularly close to any of them. They're all superficial relationships. She spends her evenings alone with her nose stuck in a book or wandering the fields behind her father's mansion.

I know that her father dotes on her when she's in his presence, but he's otherwise neglectful, staying gone a lot doing the kind of business that really burns my balls and makes the beast within me rage for blood.

Her little brows furrow as if my last statement confuses her. Hell, I guess it does. I kidnapped her, but I promised no harm would come to her.

"Where am I?" she asks, glancing around the room.

Don't ask me why I brought her to my bedroom. It's the first place I carried her limp form after my private jet landed and my driver brought us here to my home in New York.

A small part of me knows that I just wanted to see her in my bed. The feeling that swept over me when I laid her gently on my plush mattress...the way her honey-colored hair fanned out all around her on my gray bedding. She looked so innocent and tempting all at once. She looked so *right*. Like she belonged in my bed.

"My home," I answer her simply.

Her lips purse, and those chocolate eyes hold my gaze. "What state?"

She asks the question like a double question, and I know the unspoken question within her question. She wants to know if she's still in the U.S. or another country.

"New York," I answer her. I don't see the harm in letting her know what state's she's in. There's no way she'll ever be able to get away from me unless I release her.

I see some of the tension leave her shoulders at the knowledge that she's at least still on U.S. soil.

"Who are you?" she asks. She still hasn't made a move to get up from the bed. She's regarding me warily, talking slowly and evenly like I'm a beast that could turn on her at any minute. Little does she know that I might be more beast than man, but I'd never hurt her.

"Gage," I tell her my name. Again, a stupid move. I shouldn't answer any of her questions. I shouldn't tell her anything about me, much less my name, but I want to hear her say it. I want to hear my name on her lips more than I'd ever care to admit.

I know she'll say it. I know she'll have to taste my name on her lips just like I had to taste hers when I first learned it.

She doesn't disappoint me. "Gage," she says slowly, and my heart damn near jumps out of my chest at the sound. How in the hell does just my name from this girl's lips have me turned inside out? No one has ever affected me this way.

She plays with the hem of her dress, a habit she has. She does it when she's thinking or when she's nervous. In this case, I'd guess she's nervous. "When you've gotten what you want, will you let me go?"

Her big brown eyes are staring right at me, and a strand of that long hair falls over the front of her shoulder. She's wearing another little casual dress with a floral print on it. Those seem to be her favorite. Floral print dresses. She looks downright delectable in them, the tops of her pert little breasts peaking out of the scooped necklines and a generous expanse of thigh showing as the dresses fall gently several inches above her knees. I love to watch her walk in the little things, watching the hems sway back and forth, caressing her skin with each step. Her hair is slightly mussed from laying down, and if her lips were only swollen, she'd have that sinfully innocent just-fucked looked.

I feel my cock start to harden and lengthen within my pants at the thought.

Fuck, will I let her go? Will I be *able* to let her go?

She's still watching me warily, waiting for my answer, and I tell her the truth.

"I don't know, princess."

CHAPTER TWO

Ava

"NO MORE QUESTIONS," he orders as he stands to his full height in a smooth unfolding of limbs. Jesus, he's tall. His shoulders are broad and while he's not overly bulky, I can definitely tell he's nothing but muscles underneath his suit.

Dangerous. He looks so dangerous. Like a sleek, black panther.

My breath catches as he glides over to me in a smooth prowl. He stops directly before where I sit on the edge of the bed, and I have to tilt my head up to look at him.

I sit still, like the perfectly cornered prey. Just because I haven't fought him yet doesn't mean that I don't have fight within me. I'm just smart enough to know that he's at least twice my size and there's no way I can outrun him or fight him off. I'll have to outsmart him if I have any chance of escaping him. Better to play calm and meek, a complacent victim, so he underestimates me.

He said he didn't know if he was going to let me go when he gets what he wants. What does he plan on doing to me if he keeps me?

I can't let myself think about it.

His hand moves to stroke over my jawline. His touch is jarring to my entire system. It's surprisingly gentle and sends little buzzes running throughout all my nerves. I have to make a concerted effort not to flinch at his touch—or lean into it. Why the hell does a part of me want to nuzzle into his hand like a cat seeking a stroke from its master?

I don't know what the hell's wrong with me.

"The bath's that way," he nods his head in the direction of the en suite. "You should find everything you need in there. Wash up and get some sleep. I'll see you in the morning."

My heart leaps a bit in hope. He's giving me privacy. I fight the urge to ask where he'll be. I don't want to appear too eager or tip him off that I'm mentally mapping out my escape.

His hand runs down my jawline and over the expanse of my throat, sending tingles of awareness throughout my entire body. I don't know what his touch means, if it's a caress or a warning. All I know is his fingers skimming over my skin causes every bit of blood I have to rise to to the surface like there's a magnetic field pulling it to him.

I watch him carefully as his icy blue eyes follow the trail his hand makes down my neck. His expression darkens, and then he pulls his hand away, taking a step back from me.

I can finally breathe again, releasing the breath I didn't even realize I was holding.

"Are you hungry?" he asks me, clearing his throat.

I shake my head. "No, thanks."

Thanks? I mentally berate myself. What the hell am I thanking him for? He's holding me here against my will, yet I'm being polite and showing good manners for him.

He finds it odd too if the humor that sparks in his eyes and the tiny twitch of his lips are any indication. Fine, let him think I'm an idiot. It might actually work to my advantage when it's all said and done.

"Goodnight, Ava," he tells me before he walks over to the door to leave.

I can't believe my good luck. My kidnapper is acting like this is just an overnight stay. Like I'm just a guest in his home. He's not tying me up or manhandling me. Hell, he even offered me food and is giving me privacy for a shower and to sleep.

As far as kidnappings go, I'd say I lucked into the best one in the history of kidnappings.

I don't return his "goodnight." Instead, I just watch him, waiting for him to leave. He stops when he reaches the door and turns back to me with his hand still on the doorknob.

"Remember, no harm will come to you while you're under my care. There's no reason this has to be unpleasant for you. I—" he frowns before he completes his sentence, almost as if he's saying it despite his better judgement. "I want you to be comfortable."

I just stare at him, disbelieving. He seems totally serious, but I'm wondering if this is some sick game he's playing, trying to lull me into a false sense of security before he shows me what a monster he really is.

But then again, maybe he's telling the truth. He obviously wants something from my father, so maybe if he gets it, he'll just let me go.

So long as I'm good and don't piss him off and make him want to hurt me or anything.

"Okay," I nod my head at him to let him know I heard him, and then he finally leaves, closing the door behind him. I listen for the click of a lock and almost jump up and down and do a happy dance when I don't hear one.

I don't know where the hell in New York we are or how to get out of here, but I know now that I have an opportunity to try. It looks like playing it cool has paid off for me. Because I didn't give in to fits of hysteria, Gage doesn't see me as a flight risk, and I might just have a feasible chance of escape tonight.

I get up to go shower and go through the expected bedtime motions. I know I'll have to wait until I'm pretty sure he's asleep before I can put my rapidly forming plan into action.

<hr>

Gage

She thinks I've underestimated her, but what she doesn't know is that I could see the wheels turning in her head underneath her complacent little exterior.

She's smart. I'll give her that.

But, unfortunately, not as smart as me. I'm not diminishing her intelligence. I love that about her—how smart she is. But she just doesn't have the criminal and street smarts that I do.

I sit in a chair in the hall directly across from my bedroom door, waiting for her to make her move.

It's true. I was going to give her my bedroom and sleep in one of the guest bedrooms myself—all so she would be more comfortable.

But then I saw those wheels churning in her head. I knew she was going to try to run. She couldn't believe I was going to leave her alone, unsupervised. And now I can't.

I can't even say I'm disappointed. Her actions will just give me an excuse to do what I already want to do —be near her, watch over her while she sleeps.

I hear the sound of the water rushing as she takes a shower. I wonder if she's really taking one or if she's only running the water to make it seem like she is. I imagine water droplets gliding over her tanned skin, and my cock starts weeping.

I shift where I sit in the chair, adjusting my growing erection. Fuck, what would it feel like to be sheathed inside her perfection? Have that hair locked in my fists as I drive deep inside her. I've never raw dogged anyone before, but I already know there's no way I'd wear a condom with her. I'd want nothing between us.

I fist my hands on my thighs and will my erection to subside. Goddammit, I want to make her mine. She's supposed to just be a pawn to get her father to fall into line, but I already know I don't want to give her back when I've accomplished my goal.

Seeing her in my home, in my bed, it's made me want to keep her. Fuck, she looks so right here, her presence already adding something to my life. God, can I fucking keep her?

It would be so easy. So easy to keep her locked up here with me forever. I have the resources to do it, to make her disappear.

I push those dangerous thoughts away and force myself to try to keep my mind blank, to keep me from charging into that room and tunneling deep inside that pussy that's calling to me. From claiming the only girl who's ever had me knotted up like this before. From scaring the living shit out of her.

I must sit outside the door for at least two hours after the shower cuts off.

I'm under no illusions she's fallen asleep, though. My wily little princess is biding her time, waiting until she thinks *I've* fallen asleep before she makes her move.

The anticipation makes my cock harden again. Hell, every thought of Ava makes my cock hard. How the hell I'm going to keep her here for any length of time without touching her is beyond me. I refuse to be a rapist, though. And that is what it would be because I'm pretty sure she won't give herself over to her kidnapper. And I may be a criminal of the worst sort. I might be deep in the underworld, a certified bastard, but that is one line I vowed never to cross.

That's what separates me from men like Ava's piece of shit father.

I scowl, suddenly regretting my decision to kidnap her to get to her father. If I'd approached her like a normal man, would I have had a shot with her?

I guess I'll never know now.

Every muscle in my body tenses and goes on alert when I hear the soft clicking of the doorknob turning.

My eyes zone in on the door that slowly creeps open. A flash of honey-colored hair appears as Ava slowly peeks her head out the door.

Showtime.

I take a long shower, trying to kill time, and then I bide my time for a couple of hours before I dare to even walk over to the door.

I open it slowly now, peeking my head out to look up and down the hallway and get a bearing on my surroundings.

I'm so focused on looking left and right that I don't look straight ahead until I've cautiously placed one step outside the door.

"Going somewhere, Ava?"

I jump at his voice, my heart thundering up into my throat. My head swivels until my eyes connect with blue—ice blue.

His face is stoic, and he's sitting in a chair as if he expected me to try to sneak out all along. He's lost the suit jacket. Now he only wears his slacks and a button-up shirt with the sleeves rolled up to reveal muscular forearms covered in ink.

I get it now. The business suit is just a cover. A pretty veneer to hide the true beast that hides within. Just that small expanse of tatted skin shows how wild and untamed this man really is.

How severely I underestimated him. In focusing on having him underestimate me, I did the very same to him.

Damn me.

I stand there, frozen, like a deer caught in head-lights. Do I bolt? Make a run for it? Or play like I'm not trying to escape? Maybe play like I'm just venturing out to look for the kitchen?

One look into his knowing eyes, and I know he'll never buy that. It's as if he *sees* every thought flitting through my mind. Like he's omnipotent or something.

Fuck it. If I'm going down, it won't be without a fight. I've played meek so far, and look where that got me. He saw right through my bullshit.

I take off down the hallway at a sprint. I have no fucking clue where I'm going. I don't know where the entrance is. All I know is I'm running for my life.

I don't hear him behind me, but I feel him. I don't even make it to the end of the hall before his arms encircle me from behind, dragging me back against the hard planes of his chest.

He's nothing but solid muscle, a hard rock against my back. His heat is searing me from where he presses me flush against him, his arms strong and unyielding, holding me tight.

I wiggle as much as I can, trying to free myself, but it's no use. Still, I refuse to sit still, my body writhing against him with everything in me.

"Stop it, Ava," he orders, but I don't listen. I can't. I can't just relinquish my freedom.

He hisses in a sharp breath before he growls out, "So help me god, princess, I'm warning you. If you don't stop, I won't be responsible for my actions."

Something in his voice conveys to me the seriousness of his warning. As I finally calm myself and still in his arms, I finally realize what he's talking about.

My face heats when I feel something very large and very hard pressing against the small of my back. Oh god, he's turned on.

I feel so small in his hold. He's breathing raggedly in my ear, every muscle in his body still taut from the chase. His masculine scent envelopes me, intoxicating me.

I feel an answering thrum deep in my core and feel wetness begin to pool at the apex of my thighs.

God, what is wrong with me? I should be horrified to feel his raging erection pressing into my back. My mind is, but my body couldn't care less. It's responding to him on a primal level, and I hate myself for it.

I don't know how long we stand like that. Prey and predator, both perfectly still, teetering on the precipice of a cliff, until Gage finally loosens his hold on me.

"Are you going to try that again if I release you?" His deep voice is right in my ear, sending tingles up and down my spine.

I shake my head, "No. I got it out of my system."

His arms drop from around me, and my body cries at the loss of his heat while my mind is relieved to be released from his intoxicating hold.

I turn around and look up into his eyes and gasp when I see them blazing down at me. They're so bright, a vivid blue, swirling with emotions that I can't even begin to dissect.

"Come on," he orders me, motioning back to the room with his head.

I don't move, frozen in place, still staring up into his eyes.

His jaw hardens as he clenches his teeth. "Don't make me carry you, Ava."

His tone snaps me into action, and with my back ramrod straight, I walk back into the luxurious room that is now my prison.

Now that my escape attempt has failed, I'm pissed. Pissed at him for leading me to believe I was smart enough to get away. Pissed at myself for being naive enough to really think it might be this simple. Pissed at daddy for whatever he did to get on this psycho's radar.

I expect him to just sequester me off into my gilded cage before leaving me alone again. I expect him just to lock the door this time to keep me from getting out, so I stare at him in dismay when he glides into the room behind me, shutting the door.

"What are you doing?" I ask, my voice shaky.

He eyes me. "Well, I can't leave you alone now, can I? You've proven yourself untrustworthy."

My stomach plummets. "You're going to stay in here with me all night?" I croak out.

He frowns down at me. "Don't worry. I'm not into raping women. I won't touch you. In fact, I'm going to sit right here." He walks over to the chair he was sitting in when I first woke up.

"You don't have to do that," I tell him. "I'll be good now. I promise. I won't try to escape again. You can leave me alone." I'm beginning to panic at the thought of being trapped in a room with him.

"Not a chance," he answers evenly as he settles himself down into the chair.

"You can just lock me in or something," I say, trying to reason with him. My nerves won't be able to take him being in here all night.

"There's no lock on my bedroom door," he says.

Damn it, why hadn't I noticed there wasn't a lock on the door? Wait, his bedroom? This is his bedroom?

I glance around the space again, noting the masculine tone to everything and seeing it in a new light. He put me in his bed. Why would he do that if I'm just a means to an end? Why not throw me in a basement like a normal kidnapper? Nothing about him makes sense.

"Have you contacted my father yet?" The sooner my daddy gives him whatever he wants, the sooner I can get out of here. Hopefully. If he'll release me, that is. He's already admitted he might not, though why I don't know.

"Yes," he answers me unblinkingly.

I stare at him, waiting for him to elaborate, but he doesn't.

"And?" I prompt.

"And what?" he asks stoically.

I scowl at him. "How much longer am I going to be here? Is he going to give you want you want? Did you tell him you have me? I know he'll do whatever you want to get me back."

He raises a thumb up and traces it over his lower lip while he studies me. "You so sure about that?"

"What?" I bristle at the insinuation.

Gage shrugs. "I made contact with your father as soon as I had you on my plane, princess. I laid out my terms. He knows I have you. In fact, he's known it for at least eight hours now, and yet I have yet to hear back from him."

I feel the color drain from my face, but then I sputter, "He must not have gotten the message yet. He's a very busy man. He runs businesses." My father wouldn't leave me in the hands of a kidnapper. I can't believe that. There has to be a reasonable explanation for why he hasn't gotten me back yet.

Gage's face darkens. "Oh, I know all about his businesses." He practically spits the last word.

I'm quick to rush to my daddy's defense, "My father's businesses help people. He's a great man."

At that, Gage explodes, jumping up from his chair, "He's a no-good fucking snake, and he's lucky I don't kill him!"

I shrink back from his anger. I'm reminded once again that I don't know anything about this man or what he's capable of.

"Why do you hate him so much?" I whisper. "What has he ever done to you?" I can't imagine my father having anything to do with a man like this, a hardened criminal who's not above kidnapping innocent girls to get what he wants.

"It's not what he's done to me," he spits. "It's what he does to others."

I frown. I don't understand. He's implying that my father is some kind of deplorable person.

"You must have him confused with someone else—" I begin, but he cuts me off.

"He's a fucking human trafficker, Ava," he hurls down at me.

I stare up at him, my mouth open in a silent gasp. My father? A trafficker of innocent women and children? I can't believe it. I *won't* believe it.

But as soon as the denials enter my head, other thoughts creep in right after them. All the warehouses. I've never been to any of them. I've never been to any of his business locations. Agricultural investor. It's such a vague term. How do I know he really does what he says he does?

He's hardly ever home. I don't see him much at all. I never have, actually. He's always been so busy.

But when he is home, he makes me the center of his universe. He's the perfect loving father when he's around. I just can't believe the man who's spoiled me all my life could be wrapped up in something so heinous.

But if he's not, why would Gage hate him so much?

Gage's eyes soften with pity as he watches the thoughts race across my face, and that's when I *know*.

I know it's all true. He wouldn't be looking down at me with such compassion and regret if everything he just revealed was a lie.

I feel my heart crack open as my world falls apart.

"Ava," Gage begins, but I rush past him and barricade myself in the bathroom.

His bedroom might not have a lock on it, but his bathroom does, and I turn it, firmly locking out the man who single-handedly destroyed all my illusions with one sentence.

He's a fucking human trafficker.

CHAPTER THREE

Gage

FUCK ME. I didn't mean to smash her illusions of her father so coldly. It's just that I couldn't take her defense of the man. She's put him on a pedestal and idolizes him. A monster.

The truth is it makes me jealous with rage. I want her to look to *me* that way. Not him. He doesn't fucking deserve her. I don't give a fuck if he is her father. He's a piece of shit.

I try to tell myself that she would have eventually found out anyway, but something inside me says I still shouldn't have blurted it out in a fit of jealous rage over her defense of him.

I try the door on the bathroom, but unsurprisingly, it's locked. She's barricaded herself inside.

"Ava," I say softly but firmly. "Open the door."

Silence.

I grit my teeth. I'm not a man who's used to being ignored, and I'm already strung tight over my fuck up with her. I want to try to make it right if I can, but I can't do fuck all if she keeps herself locked up in there all night.

"I'm only going to tell you one more time, princess," I try to keep my voice low and even as I speak to her, "Open the door."

Silence again.

I clench my teeth together so hard I'm surprised I don't break my jaw.

"Ava, if you don't open this goddamned door, I swear to fuck I'll break it down."

I finally see the doorknob turn, and the door slowly opens to reveal her small frame standing there, her eyes downcast. She's allowing her hair to fall on either side of her face, effectively hiding behind it.

"Look at me," I tell her.

She makes no move to lift her head, so I reach out a hand and gently cup her chin, lifting her face up.

Fuck me. It's like a punch to the gut. Her eyes are red-rimmed and glistening with tears. They're filled with sadness and confusion, and a surge of protectiveness swells up within me. I want to kill whatever asshole made her feel this way, and then I realize that asshole is me.

Fuuuck.

But it's her father too. Her fucking human trafficking piece of shit father. I hate him. I hate him for what he does. I hate him for deceiving me. I hate him for hurting his sweet daughter this way.

Of its own volition, my thumb strokes over her cheek. Her skin is petal soft. She's so delicate and fragile. And Christ but her tear-stained face is beautiful. I never want to see her crying, but somehow those tears make her even more beautiful.

Or maybe I'm just fucked in the head. Hell, I don't know. All I know is she's the most gorgeous thing I've ever fucking seen, and I'm quickly losing sight of my goal in all this. Yes, I still want to see Sinclair pay for what he's done, but I also want his daughter.

I want Ava as my own. *Mine. Mine. Mine.* The mantra chants in time with my heavy heartbeat in this silence that stretches between us as she looks up at me sadly with shimmering moisture in her eyes. I gaze down at her, trying to figure out how I can keep her without her hating me.

I'm trying to think of what to say, but nothing seems sufficient. I've never been struck speechless before, but this girl's tears have done just that. Another human being has never had such power over me before.

It's a foreign sensation that I both love and hate.

But then she shocks the hell out of me when she suddenly wraps her arms around my waist and burrows her face against my chest, sobbing, her thin shoulders shaking with her grief.

My arms instantly circle around her, holding her close. I stroke her hair, murmuring words of comfort to her. "It'll be okay, princess. I'll never let anything hurt you. I'm so sorry, Ava. I'm so sorry."

I don't know if she hears me. She continues to cry, clinging to me like I'm her lifeline. I'd be lying if I said I'm not secretly loving every minute of it. I hate that she's in pain, but my soul soars that she turned to me for comfort. Maybe it's because she's somewhat in shock or just that I'm the only other living, breathing organism around for her to cling to when she needs solace, but I don't give a fuck either way.

I held her in my arms before, but it's different now that she sought me out of her own accord. She initiated this touch. She's lucid in my arms, and it's the best fucking feeling in the world to have her there.

I never want to let her go.

I'm stroking up and down her back, and I feel her soothing underneath my touch. Her body goes lax against me, pressing into mine, and her sobs begin to quiet.

I'm dangerously hard, my cock like a slab of marble in my pants. Every muscle in my body is tense with the effort it takes to control myself, to keep from grabbing handfuls of her delicious little ass and lifting her up until she wraps those beautiful fucking legs around me.

I've never wanted to put my dick in a woman so bad before in all my life.

She squirms against me, sending fire through my loins with the friction she creates. I tighten my arms around her, holding her still. I close my eyes tightly and breathe in slowly through my nostrils, attempting to calm my raging libido. There's a primal animal instinct within me. It's throbbing between my legs, telling me to claim, claim, claim. "Don't move," I croak out.

Of course she doesn't fucking listen. She squirms against me again, lifting her head to look up at me with beautifully tear-swollen eyes. Her hands slide around to my chest, and her little pink lips open, and that does it.

I detonate.

I grab her hands in mine, holding them against my chest as I crash my lips down on hers. Once I have my lips against hers, my hands come up to frame her face, holding her still for my assault.

Her shocked gasp gives me easy entrance to the haven of her mouth, and I stroke my tongue wildly against hers, tasting her sweetness, sucking on her puffy lips. I crush her against my chest and feel her nipples harden against me.

Fucking fuck. Her body is responding to me.

Her inexperience is obvious, leading me to believe she's never even been kissed before, and that really fucks with my head. I'm so turned on, I'm almost high with lust. When she tentatively begins to move her tongue against mine, kissing me back, I swear every ounce of blood in my body rushes south to the monster between my legs.

I've never come so undone over a kiss before. In all honestly, I've never been into kissing much before, preferring to keep distance between me and my part-ners. But fuck, with Ava? I want it all. I want to kiss every inch of her.

I kiss my way from her lips down over the

delectable column of her throat. She tips her head back, granting me easier access, and then I feel her little fingers spear into my hair.

I lick and suck behind the shell of her ear, breathing hotly against the lobe, and she shivers against me, letting out a little pant that drives me fucking wild.

I hold her firmly against my chest with one hand on the small of her back and explore her body with the other one. My hand grazes over the swell of her breast before continuing its journey down and over her bare thigh until I reach the sweet juncture between her legs.

Her panties are soaked. Fucking soaked.

I feel a jet of precum shoot from my cock in response, painting the inside of my boxer briefs with sticky fluid.

"Fuck, princess, fuck," I whisper. All my earlier reservations about touching her have gone out the window with her body's response to me.

I yank down the top of her dress, revealing her pert tits and begin to feast on them, flicking my tongue over the hardened nubs. Her erratic breathing is music to my ears, and her gasp when I suckle one of the buds into my mouth almost makes me come in my pants. I swear to Christ I could explode just from the sound of her moans alone. She's so goddamned sexy, she doesn't even know.

My fingers stroke her through her wet panties while I worship her tits, coating my fingers in her sweet juices until I know I have to have a taste.

I drop to my knees before her and fist her dress around her waist as I put my nose between her legs and inhale deeply, learning the scent of her.

"Gage," her voice is wobbly and uncertain, only reaffirming my suspicions that no one else has ever been between her legs like this before. The joy that knowledge gives me...that I'm the only man to ever be this close to her pussy...

"Just one taste, baby," I tell her, my voice thick with lust, before I move her panties to the side and lave her gash with my tongue. Her sweetness explodes on my tongue like the finest elixir.

Peaches and cream. She tastes like fucking peaches and cream.

I can't stop the possessive growl that comes from my throat as I begin to lick her in earnest. I want more. I want her dripping on my face.

I quickly find her clit and begin to bat at it with my tongue.

Her legs shake around me, and her hands fist in my

hair as she struggles, half trying to move away, half canting her hips into my face.

I palm her ass cheeks with my hands, holding her still as I latch onto her swollen little nub and begin to suckle it in a soft rhythm meant to drive her wild.

It does if her gasps and whimpers are any indication. I worship her pussy with everything in me. I've never tasted anything so incredible. Her responses of pleasure are only amplifying the experience. My cock is leaking a steady stream of precum now. I can't hold it all in.

"Gage, it's too much!" she finally cries, almost sobbing in distress. I know she's close. I work a finger into her cunt and can feel the muscles of her pussy contracting in the first tremors of an impending orgasm. I push my finger up into her until I hit the thin barrier that is her hymen. I almost pass out with the surge of lust that fills me at finally knowing for sure she's a virgin. My finger retreats. My cock will be the first thing to pierce that barrier while I'm staring down into her gorgeous brown eyes.

I latch onto her clit and suck hard while swirling my tongue around it, and she screams.

I glance up at her to see her head thrown back, her skin flushed from her face down to her exposed tits as the orgasm rocks her body. I've never seen a more erotic sight. I feel her pussy tightening and releasing around my finger, and my cock is jealous.

I continue to lap at her, drinking up every bit of juices flowing from her sweet, virgin hole.

I feel the tell-tale tightening in my balls and can't believe I'm about to come just from watching this sweet angel orgasm.

"Motherfucker," I groan as I yank my cock out of my pants and grip my length to keep myself from exploding.

I stagger to my feet, cock in my tightly held fist as I catch Ava with one hand when she begins to crumble against me.

I can't hold it any longer. I feel my cum rising up through my shaft, so still holding onto her waist, I take one step back and give myself one pump.

One stroke of my fist over my engorged length. That's all it takes before I see stars as I feel my seed ripping from me. I hear it splatter against the skin of her stomach where I still have her dress held up.

She stares up at me slack-jawed, still flushed and lax from her own orgasm as I continue to ejaculate all over her, painting her abdomen with the evidence of my desire for her.

When I'm done, my shoulders slump, and I damn near fall to the floor. The only thing keeping me standing upright is the knowledge that I have to keep her from falling.

I look down at her. Her breasts are still hanging from the top of her dress, her white cotton panties are still pushed to the side, revealing her glorious mound. Her hair is falling all around her shoulders. Her lips are swollen from my kisses. Her stomach is covered in my spunk.

She's disheveled and so fucking beautiful.

I should probably wipe my seed off her, but bastard that I am, I love seeing it on her. Love knowing that it's there. So instead, I reach out a hand and rub it into her skin like it's a sticky moisturizer.

She still doesn't say a word. She's just standing there in shock, watching me with that wide-eyed innocence that cripples me.

Fuck, I should be ashamed of myself, but I'm not. I can't regret tasting her sweet heaven, making her come on my tongue, marking her with my cum.

I see the confusion and questions in her eyes, but still she doesn't speak. That's for the best. Words would only complicate what just happened here. I'm not ready for them yet. She's not ready for them yet.

So, wordlessly, I slip her dress off over her head. Like a limp doll, she lets me, her eyes never leaving mine.

Then I bend down and scoop her up into my arms, cradling her against me.

I carry her over to my bed and lay her gently on it, pulling the covers up around her.

I tuck her in still dripping in my cum.

Ava

Oh. My. God.

I can't believe what just happened.

I watch from where I'm laying as Gage disappears into the bathroom. His pants were still open when he carried me over to his bed, revealing a male specimen that's still very large even when it's flacid.

Did I really just let my kidnapper give me my first orgasm?

What the holy fuck is wrong with me?

Shame and guilt engulf me, and my face burns with the memory of his head between my legs.

And I can't even say he forced me or anything. I turned to him for comfort.

Why?

All I know is upon finding out the horrible truth

about my father, I'd been devastated, so I reached out for the only source of comfort within reach.

It's been so long since anyone held me or comforted me. Has anyone since Mom? My father dotes on me when he's around, but he keeps his distance physically. I can't even remember the last time he hugged me.

So what does this mean? That I'm so attention-starved that I seek solace in the arms of the man who means me harm?

But wait, that's not right. Gage doesn't mean me harm. On the contrary, he promised me that no harm would come to me while I was with him.

My head is spinning with confusion. Our kidnapper-victim dynamic is seriously fucked up.

The bathroom door clicks open, and Gage comes striding out, only now he's wearing nothing but his boxer briefs.

My heart rate ticks up a notch. I can now see all the ink covering one full arm and some of his chest. His muscles are hard and well-defined, and I can't keep my eyes from trailing down over them to the V that disappears beneath his boxers.

The man is a god. Sculpted from marble, he can't be of this world. He's dangerously handsome, and I feel my cheeks flame again when my eyes finally flick back up to his face to find those ice blue eyes piercing me again.

I pull the covers closer to me under my chin to cover my nudity as he closes the space between us.

It's no use, though, because with one motion, he effectively pulls it from my grasp. Then, he slips into the bed beside me, laying on his side. He arranges me on my side before pulling me back against him, my back flush against his chest, his heavy arm wrapped firmly around me.

The only thing separating us is his boxers and my panties.

And I feel how long and thick that part of him is again. I don't even want to think about what that means or my body's traitorous response to him.

I lay there stiffly, too embarrassed to say a word. I've just gone further with my kidnapper than any boyfriend I've ever had.

My mind races. What is he doing? Does he really intend to spoon with me all night?

"Relax, Ava." His voice is hot against my ear. "We're just going to sleep."

"Sleep?" I repeat stupidly.

I can hear the amusement in his tone when he answers. "Yes, unless you want to engage in other activities."

"No," I answer quickly. "I'm good."

He chuckles, the vibrations from his chest echoing into my back. God, he's so huge, completely wrapped around me like this. There's no way I can go anywhere if I try. And I suddenly realize that's probably the point of this. It's the only way he can sleep and ensure I don't slip away—short of tying me up or doing any of the normal things kidnappers do, which for some reason, he seems averse to doing.

I just know I'm not going to be able to sleep with this hulk of a man wrapped around me, but after a while, his warm body heat begins to feel comforting. As much as I hate to admit it, I like the feel of his full-body hug. Oddly enough, I feel safe in his embrace, and that's the most fucked-up thing of all.

He's the one I need saving from.

CHAPTER FOUR

Gage

I DON'T KNOW how long she battles with her conflicting thoughts, but eventually, I feel her body go lax against me as my body heat lulls her to sleep.

It's obvious what she was thinking. She's struggling with the thought that her kidnapper made her come. She wants to hate me, and I'm sure a part of her does, but her body responds to me.

I'm not fitting into the typical kidnapper mold. I'm not being the monster she expects me to be, and it's fucking with her mind.

Hell, she's not the only one. My response to her is

fucking with me too. I shouldn't be this tender with her. I shouldn't have this crazed need to coddle her and protect her. But I do. At the same time, I want to possess her. I want to own every part of her. Mind, heart, body, and soul. I want her to crave me the way I crave her.

As if my obsession can't get any worse, now that I've tasted her, I only want more. Like a junkie, one hit isn't enough. I know that every time I hold her, it'll only strengthen my desire for her, and I'll have to keep having more and more to keep myself sane.

I'm trying to ignore the erection between my legs. It'd be so easy to rip those flimsy little panties from her body and stuff my aching staff inside her. God knows I need the relief. Badly.

My release on her stomach earlier barely took the edge off my lust. Now it's back in full force, tormenting me as I hold the sweetest body in the world in my arms.

I can't help tilting my head down and inhaling deeply, breathing in her sweet scent.

She feels so tiny and frail in my arms. So breakable. So vulnerable. It brings out a protective rush in me.

She's mine. Mine to hold. Mine to protect. I'm not even going to fucking fight it anymore. I don't care. I don't care if it doesn't make sense. I'm not going to be able to let her go. I know that now.

I haven't even fucked her yet, and every part of me aches at the thought of not having her here with me.

She stirs in my arms, rolling toward me in her sleep and nuzzling her little head closer to me, burrowing into my chest.

My chest tightens at her subconscious movement. I've never let a woman get close enough to me before to sleep with me, to cuddle into me like this. It's an amazing feeling coming from this girl. This sweet, innocent, little angel.

I stroke her hair, petting her like she's a sleeping kitten.

I don't sleep. I stare down at her all night, marveling at this beauty in my arms. I don't want to miss a moment of watching her. I'm relieved to see that her dreams must be peaceful. Her face is soft in sleep, her little pink lips at ease. Any time she does toss, it's to move closer to me.

I realize it's probably a form of madness, the way I can stare at her all night so contentedly, but I really don't give a fuck. I passed the point of no return the moment I tasted the peaches and cream from her pretty pink pussy.

I'm irritated when my buzzing phone draws my

attention away from her. I don't get to watch her slowly wake up because she's jolted awake by both my movements and the infernal noise from the phone.

She quickly scoots away from me like I have leprosy, pulling the covers up to her chin as a shield. I try to ignore the pang of hurt at both her actions and the suspicious, disdainful look she throws my way.

"Morelli," I snap my surname in greeting when I flick open my phone.

"Gage," Sinclair's smooth voice comes over the line. "I understand you have my daughter?" He doesn't ask to see or speak to her. Sinclair knows I'm a man of my word. If I say I have his daughter, I've got her.

I grit my teeth at the familiarity of him using my first name. Then, I notice there's none of the panic in his voice that most men would have at a man like me having their daughter in his possession. No, Sinclair just states the question like he's asking about the weather or a business merger.

"Have you gone over my terms?" I ask him in a bored, cold tone that should let him know I mean business.

I feel Ava's eyes trained on me, but she doesn't say a word. She doesn't scream or plead to speak with her father, even though she has to have figured out that's who I'm on the phone with by now.

"Ah, yeah, uh, see, that's the thing..." The first hints of nervousness lace his voice. His voice lowers conspiratorially as if he's confessing some great secret. "I don't have that kind of cash yet, and I won't if you force me to shut down my business."

"I'm sorry I didn't fully disclose the details to you earlier, Morelli," the man goes on. "I didn't really think it was important," he lies.

"Come now, Sinclair," my voice is deceptively calm. "You knew I wouldn't front you the money if I'd known it was for human trafficking. Don't play me for a fool. It's not befitting a man of your stature."

Sinclair laughs nervously and tries to play off the precarious position he's in. "Come on, Morelli. You've got your hands in everything in the underworld. It's a lucrative business."

My hand grips the phone so tightly I'm surprised I don't shatter it. "There are some lines even I won't cross. But apparently there's no end to your stupidity. Did you really think you could blindside me with something like this and come out unscathed?"

"What are you going to do with Ava?" the man finally shows a sliver of concern for his daughter.

I ignore his question. "I want my money in full by the end of the day, and shut that operation down."

Sinclair is silent a long moment before he finally answers. "That's impossible."

"You know what happens to men who don't play by my rules, Sinclair," I state matter-of-factly. Yes, I know what I'm asking is impossible. He knows why I made it so too. He knows I'm coming for him no matter what.

"Ava," Sinclair finally offers in a panic. "Keep Ava. She can cover the debt, and I'll work on shutting everything down."

I glance over at the topic of our conversation. She's still sitting as far away from me on the bed as she can manage with the covers pulled tight up under her chin, staring at me with wide eyes.

The pained look on her face lets me know that she heard what her father offered over the phone.

I hate Sinclair with every fiber of my being in this moment. That he would barter with his precious daughter like this, give her over to who he presumes is a monster, a man who for all he knows will do terrible things to her. He's willing to trade her life for his own. The fucking slime ball.

I'm outraged on her behalf. If the man were sitting here in front of me, I'd break his jaw.

Still, that doesn't stop me from taking the only thing I've ever really wanted.

"Done," I tell him.

———

Ava

My father doesn't make any requests for Gage to be gentle with me. He doesn't even ask anything about what Gage plans to do with me after he signs my life away to him.

He just gives me away. Just like that.

The final nail in my coffin. The last vestige of the illusion of the father I never really had gone.

Had he ever truly given a shit about me? Or, was it all just him playing the part of the doting father because it made him look good to the senators and other business associates he had over to the house?

Gage never takes his eyes off me as he hangs up the phone. He's looking at me with that same look of pity he wore when he first told me the truth about my father, and I can't take it.

I. Can. Not. Take. It.

"Ava," he begins, but I can't.

I can't sit here and listen to a word he has to say.

Clutching the covers around me, I jump up from the bed and make a mad dash for the door. I don't know where I think I'm going. I'm just acting on instinct. And my instincts are telling me to get as far away from this man as I can before I break down and start sobbing in his arms again.

He's on me in less than three seconds, hauling me back against his hard chest. I thrash and kick in his hold, all while still managing to keep my grip on the cover to keep from exposing my naked breasts to him. "Let me go!" I scream.

"No," he answers calmly. "You're mine now."

"I will never be yours," I hiss at him vehemently.

He doesn't argue as he pins my arms to my sides with one strong arm around my chest. He holds me like that for several moments until my heart rate calms down and I expend my energy, my muscles easing as my senses come back to me, the realization that fighting this man is fruitless. I will never beat him in a physical contest. He will overpower and dominate me every time.

When I finally stop fighting him, he turns me in his arms to face him, still holding me tight against him with an arm around the small of my back, pressing my hips into him.

He forces me to look up at him with a finger to my chin. "I'm sorry," he says, looking down at me tenderly.

"I don't understand what kind of father would trade his daughter to settle his debt."

I stare up at him incredulously before saying, "The same kind of man who would accept said daughter for payment of a debt."

His brows instantly furrow. "Your father and I are *not* the same. I'll take care of you, Ava," he adds earnestly. "I'd never give you away."

"I'm not a possession to be bartered and traded among men," I scoff.

"I don't see you that way." His blue eyes burn down into mine.

"No?" I raise an eyebrow at him. "You took me to get leverage over my father. Then, you accepted his offer to keep me to settle whatever the beef is between you and him. You claim you're so against human trafficking, which, by definition, is the kidnapping, buying, and selling of human beings, yet that's exactly what you've done to me. You're no different from him."

He releases me and steps back from me like I've slapped him. His body recoils as if I've physically hit him. I push away the stab of remorse that hits me. Damn it, it's true. He *did* kidnap me. He *did* accept me as payment. Like I'm a thing—not a person.

He frowns down at me for a long moment before

he finally speaks. "Go get cleaned up." He motions to the bathroom.

I grit my teeth, balking at the notion of being ordered around like a pet.

The *only* reason why I turn on my heel and go to obey is because I can't wait to take a shower and wash his cum and all evidence of his touch off my body.

***

Gage

I watch her as she stalks to the bathroom, taking all the covers with her. Despite the fact that I feasted on those tits and was nose-deep in her pussy yesterday, she still feels the need to hide her body from me.

I'm completely unsurprised when I hear the loud click of the lock being turned like she snapped it ferociously into place. If I wasn't so knifed by her brutal comparison of me to her father, I'd be amused.

As if a lock could keep me out. As if *anything* could keep me from her if I wanted her.

Her accusations sting. I don't want to see the truth in her words because the real truth is I would never do anything to hurt her. I just want to keep her here with me. I want to take care of her and give her the world. Is that so wrong?

I pinch the bridge of my nose in irritation before stalking over to my closet and pulling on a pair of sweatpants. I pull out another pair with a drawstring and one of my smallest shirts—one of the ones that's tight on me.

A better man would release her, but I've never claimed to be a good man, so I'm keeping Ava. In time, she'll come to see that I won't harm her. That I only want to give her pleasure and make her happy.

I pull the knife I from my discarded slacks from last night and make quick work of picking the bathroom lock.

Ava doesn't even see me when I slip into the bathroom and hang the clothes on the hooks. She's turned facing away from the door, holding her head up to the spray of the water.

My cock instantly hardens at the sight of her naked body with water drizzling down it. The reality of my fantasies yesterday is even more beautiful in person.

I clench my hands into fists, trying to restrain myself. It would be so easy to slip into the shower with her, come up behind her, grab her around the throat, and sheath myself inside her slick, hot heat. I can already hear the wet slapping of our bodies as I thrust into her and find release, marking her as mine.

And just like that, I feel precum moistening the tip of my cock.

With great effort, I back out of the bathroom and close the door behind me. Breathing heavily, I stand behind the closed bathroom door and slowly count to ten, willing my raging hard-on to subside.

I want her to learn to trust me. I want her to want me as badly as I want her. In order to do that, I can't just take her in the shower—however badly I may want to.

I also still have businesses to run, so as much as I might want to babysit her all day, I know I won't be able to do that either.

My pretty little bird is going to need a gilded cage.

CHAPTER FIVE

Ava

IT BOTH DISTURBS and relieves me to see clothes hanging up for me when I get out of the shower. I'm disturbed because Gage must have picked the lock and come in to put them there because they certainly weren't there when I got into the shower.

I'm relieved because it means that Gage was in here unbeknownst to me. He could have done anything to me, yet he didn't. I don't know why that relieves me so much. On some basic level, I somehow know he won't hurt me. If he was going to do that, he's had plenty of opportunity to do so.

I put on what are obviously *his* clothes. Even with pulling the drawstring of his sweats as far as it will go, the pants want to hang off my hips. Fortunately, the shirt is long enough to cover my exposed hips. It's so long, in fact, that it comes down to my knees. The way the clothing swamps me only serves to remind me that my captor is not a small man by any means.

When I emerge from the bathroom clean and dressed, he's waiting there for me. He's dressed in sweatpants too—nothing but sweatpants. I instantly avert my eyes. Even though I slept with all that hard muscle curled around me all night, it seems somehow different to see it all on display so close up in the light of day.

The man is gorgeous. There's not an ounce of fat on him. The tattoos that I'd only glimpsed under his rolled-up shirtsleeves only heighten his attractiveness, adding to his dark allure. I want to study each one, but I won't allow myself to look. This is not the reaction I'm supposed to be having to him.

Him. The man who kidnapped me. Who's holding me here against my will. Who decided to accept me as payment for a debt. I feel the anger roiling up in me again and force myself to stand straighter at the thought, crossing my arms over my chest.

I refuse to make this easy on him. In fact, I'll make

him so damn miserable, he'll have no choice to but to let me go.

To my surprise he chuckles.

I glance up at him sharply.

"It won't work," he says softly, grinning down at me like I'm a recalcitrant child.

"What won't?" I ask him.

"What you're thinking." His grin widens.

"You have no idea what I'm thinking," I scoff.

"I won't get pissed enough at you to let you go. And I won't get bored with you. So, let's just skip the part where you determine to make my life a living hell and end up only making it harder on yourself."

I glare at him, wishing I had a knife—anything—to stab him with and wipe that smug smirk off his face.

"Come on," he says before I can say anything.

"Where are you taking me?" I ask suspiciously before allowing myself to move to follow him. I will not be a willing captive.

His blue eyes pierce me with a sudden intense light. "To your new room."

Ava

He moves me out of his bedroom. I'm glad for that. I really am. If I'm no longer stuck in his bedroom, then I shouldn't have to endure his hulking form wrapped around me at night.

Besides, why would he want to keep me in his bedroom forever? It's not like we're a couple or anything. I'm his captive. A slave, basically. Nothing more.

Of course, the new room he moved me to has a lock on it—from the outside, though, which means that he can lock me in here when he goes away, which of course I'm sure was the whole point of moving me here.

I really can't complain about the room, though. It's just as luxurious as his was—if in a softer way. This room gives off a gentler vibe. It's not as masculine as his room was, but there's still a huge en suite bathroom and even a spacious sitting room with shelves of books to read to keep me occupied during the day.

I suppose my captivity could be worse.

After he deposits me in my new room, he leaves, telling me has business to attend to but that he'll see me later.

I just stare at him stonily, not giving him the pleasure of a response.

I'm already trying to plot my escape from him. I

have no idea how I'll manage it, but it will become my life's mission to do so.

I prowl every inch of my new cage, looking for any weaknesses. Unsurprisingly, I find none. Frustrated, I plop onto the plush sofa and groan.

I won't allow myself to think of my father. The moment he traded me to save his own ass he died to me. I refuse to shed tears over a father I never really knew. Everything about him was a lie. My heart aches at the thought. Was he always like that, or had it all happened after my mother died?

I'll never know, and it doesn't matter now. I *won't* allow myself to think of him.

Instead, I spend the morning stewing until a man comes to the room to give me a tray of food. My stomach betrays me by growling loudly, but I ignore it and try to solicit the man's help.

It's no use, though. No matter how much I try to tell him I need help, that I'm being held here against my will, he just looks away and asks if I need anything else.

He won't even acknowledge my plight. There's no telling what Gage pays this butler for his loyalty.

I consider trying to barrel past him out the door, but his hulking frame is almost as big as Gage's, and I'm not naive enough to think that he's only a servant.

This man is a guard too. I'm sure one of his duties is to make sure I don't leave this estate.

I eat my food resignedly after he leaves. I have to begrudgingly admit that it's some of the best food I've ever tasted. The crepes are light and fluffy, and the tomatoes are fresh and juicy. I swear the orange juice is fresh-squeezed, and the coffee tastes like a gourmet roast.

After I finish eating, I sit there for a moment contemplating my options. I can keep sitting here making myself miserable, or I can grab a book from one of the many shelves and try to forget about my problems and lose myself in another world.

Eventually, I opt for the latter option, selecting a historical fiction novel about life in the Old West. I become so engrossed in its pages that I don't look up until I hear the door open again.

The same man from before comes in bearing a tray of lunch, and he's followed by a woman pushing a rack of clothing through the door. The man brings me my tray while the woman heads over to the closet and wordlessly begins loading it up.

My stomach sinks within me. As if I needed any more proof that this is real, that this is really happening, seeing that my captor has funded me a full wardrobe only reinforces the notion that he plans on keeping me for a long time—forever even.

"What are your names?" I ask the man and woman, but they both keep to their tasks as if I haven't said a word.

So they've been forbidden to talk to me outside providing for my basic needs then.

I try to ask them more questions, but they continue to act like they don't hear me.

I finally give up and give them the silent treatment back, going back to my book and ignoring them as they continue stocking the piles upon piles of clothes in the closet.

Jesus, how many clothes does he think I need? Especially if he's going to keep me locked up in here? Out of the corner of my eye, I see some gorgeous dresses and even some frilly lingerie, and my face heats in anger. If he thinks he's going to keep me caged up and I'm going to dress up all nice and pretty for him every day, he's out of his fucking mind.

I make a mental note then and there to dress in the drabbest shit I can find daily.

Fuck him.

Gage

I don't plan on keeping Ava caged up forever, but just like I knew she would, she's trying to plot ways to freedom. I'm hoping that after enough time passes she'll see it's futile and give it up. That maybe she'll even grow to be happy here when she sees what all I can give her and what all I'll do for her.

Jose and Rosa have already reported back to me about how she's tried to solicit their help, which lets me know if I took her out in public right now she'd no doubt do the same of any passerby.

I don't begrudge her for trying it. It's only natural. What would be unnatural is if she accepted her fate without qualm.

Still, I can't help but yearn for the day when all this is behind us and she accepts what is and begins to open up to me.

Because that's what's going to happen.

As it is, I'm trying to give her space. As much as it kills me and goes against everything in me, I'm letting her sleep alone in her own room, giving her time to acclimate to her new life.

I force myself to go to work, leaving her alone for

hours on end in her room. Though I can't trust her enough yet to give her access to any sort of communications devices, I did have a TV installed in her room with every channel in the sky on it. And she has shelves upon shelves of books to read. I know that's where her real passion lies.

Although Jose and Rosa know better than to get too friendly with her right now (I've forbidden them from speaking to her in any context other than attending to her needs for the time being) they watch her accordingly and have informed me that she rarely turns the TV on, spending most of her time with her nose in a book.

I'm not purposefully being cruel by denying her human contact. It's just that when she takes solace from her loneliness, I want it to be with me.

She's harder to crack than I thought she'd be, though. It's been two weeks, and she still speaks barely two words to me when I I go to see her every night.

Well, in the beginning she tried to negotiate her way out of her captivity. She promised she'd never tell about the kidnapping. She'd forget everything. When she finally realized her pleas were falling on deaf ears, she switched tactics.

The silent treatment.

She thinks it bothers me, and she's right. I'd much

rather she talk to me. I don't just want a living doll. I want her. All of her. But what she doesn't understand is I have way more patience than she does. Plus, I'm content to take her however I can get her. I can sit in her room all night just staring at her as she pretends to read like she doesn't even know I'm there. What she doesn't realize is that I can see her reading the same lines over and over again in her frustration. My presence isn't as easy to ignore as she likes to make out.

She begrudgingly started wearing the clothes I bought her after she stubbornly stayed in my clothes for three days. What she fails to realize is I couldn't give a fuck less what she wears. She's beautiful to me regardless, and call me a primate, but it gives me a primal sense of pleasure to see her drowning in *my* clothes anyway, so her unwillingness to take them off at first had only fueled my desire for her.

Still, I notice she tries to find the least sexy stuff to wear, but the stylist I hired was good and every piece— even the fashionably oversized off-the-shoulder tees and leggings fit Ava perfectly and only enhance her beauty.

She hasn't touched any of the makeup, and she leaves her hair down every day. She simply brushes it out after her shower and lets it air dry.

It doesn't matter. She's breathtaking au naturale

and doesn't need any makeup and fancy hairstyles. With her thick eyelashes and naturally rosy lips, she's a man's wet dream.

And I'm no saint, so boy do I have them—wet dreams, that is. It doesn't matter how many times I stroke myself off, I wake up every night with an aching cock. Time and again I find myself tempted to make myself to her room and finally take her, but I won't let myself do that.

When I take Ava, it won't be by force. When I finally slip into her heavenly depths and make her mine in every way, it'll be because she wants it as much as I do. I'll make her admit it before I give us what our bodies both so desperately crave.

"Good evening, princess," I greet her as I always do, strolling into her room after getting home from attending to some business. "How was your day?"

I might deal with business of the more unsavory sort, but it's a full-time job—maybe even more so than legitimate business. There are always infractions to deal with and new opportunities to flesh out.

I didn't realize how dark my existence was before Ava. Usually, I'd come home to this huge, empty estate and do even more work from my home office before having a drink and calling it a night.

Now, I look forward to coming home to her every day. She's the light in my dark world.

Even with her glowering at me like this.

She has on an oversized burgundy top that brings out the honey streaks in her hair and deepens her brown eyes to rich mocha.

Fuck, she looks so fresh and beautiful. I know if I just lifted that shirt up, I'd find her ripe little ass so pert and full in those little black leggings.

My cock immediately rises to attention in my slacks.

This is the effect she has on me. I don't even have to touch her. Just being in her presence is enough to put all my senses on alert and have my cock aching for her.

I don't know if I can hold off much longer.

"Kidnap anyone new today?" She tilts her head, her hair falling over the front of her shoulder in a silky motion, her voice falsely sweet.

I grin at her, triumphant to have gotten even this sarcastic bit of communication from her. "Of course not, princess. And don't worry. No one could ever take your place."

Her false smile instantly sours into a scowl, and I chuckle. Of course, I want her willing and smiling up at me for real one day, but for now, I can't deny that I enjoy sparring with her and getting a rise out of her. The way her cheeks flush in anger and indignation, the way her little fists ball in pent-up fury, the way her eyes glitter and her little jaw sets.

She's adorable in all her fury.

I walk over to her and place a chaste kiss on her forehead. I can't help it. I have to touch her in some small way today. Though I want to kiss so much more, I make myself stop at the press of my lips to her forehead. Any more and I won't be able to stop myself.

It's just as well because her little hands are instantly pressing against my chest, pushing me away.

"Don't touch me!" she hisses like a kitten with its hackles up.

I put my hands up in surrender, but I'm smiling down at her.

No matter how angry she acts, I still felt her body's response to me. I felt the full-body tremor that went through her when my lips touched her skin. I still see the flush in her cheeks and can practically hear her heart thumping in tune with mine.

Ava's body is already mine. I'm just waiting for her mind.

CHAPTER SIX

Ava

GAGE COMES in to see me like he does every day after he gets home from whatever the hell it is a criminal does all day. I hate myself for secretly looking forward to his visits every day, but he's the only real human contact I have. The servants are only quickly in and out to bring me food and other necessities, and I quickly figured out they won't speak to me at all unless it's concerning something of that nature.

I don't have Stockholm Syndrome, but Gage has effectively made himself the center of my universe—hell, the *only* one in my sphere—and I hate him for it.

I hate him for making me crave his presence. Even when he just sits there and stares at me while I ignore him, it's better than sitting here alone.

I try not to speak to him much. I don't want to grow any closer to him. I want him to get bored with me and let me go.

None of it seems to be working, though.

He comes every night like clockwork, charging the air with his electricity, though he rarely touches me beyond a gentle finger on my face or a chaste press of his lips to my forehead.

I instantly know something is different tonight, though, when he comes through the door with more agitation than usual. The air around him is crackling with energy, but he addresses me the same as usual, greeting me as his princess and asking how my day has been.

And I treat him the same as usual, pointedly ignoring him and continuing to read, though my hands are shaking so much that I drop the pretty, tassled bookmark I'm holding behind the open book.

That's another thing. Not only did Gage make sure to stock this room with all the types of books I like to read, but I also woke up one day to find an assortment of gorgeous bookmarks on display by the shelves. I don't know how he did it, but it's like he somehow crawled into my mind and learned all my preferences and then started fulfilling them.

It only makes it that much harder to hate him, which, ironically, only makes me hate him even more.

It's complicated.

I can't reach the bookmark from where I'm sitting on the couch, so I stand and then bend over to pick it up.

Only when I rise and turn back around, holding the book open to the page I'm reading with a finger pressed between the pages and the bookmark clutched in the other hand do I realize my error.

Gage's hungry gaze is trained on my legs, and my face heats as his piercing blue eyes travel up my body to meet my own eyes.

My fingers curl tighter around the bookmark and my breath hitches when I see what can only be described as animal lust in his eyes.

Damn it, damn it, damn it!

This fucking dress. I knew better than to wear one of the little floral dresses that looked so much like something I'd pick out myself I could almost believe it came from my own closet back home.

But I've run out of oversized shirts and leggings to wear. It's like Gage is purposefully denying me washed clothes because once the maid takes something away for cleaning, I never see it again.

I figure it's his way of eliminating my choices until I'm forced to wear the sexier, more revealing items he bought me.

I forgot about the fucking dress, and in bending over, I no doubt gave him a nice flash of my ass in the cheeky panties I put on this morning. Yes, I'm down to the cheekies now. My panty supply is dwindling as well. I'm two cheekies away from a thong, and I've never been a fan of those. A man obviously invented the thong because no woman in her right mind would think it's a good idea to stick a string up her ass and call it coverage.

Although judging by the look on Gage's face, my cheekies don't offer much coverage either.

He begins to stalk over to me, and I take a step back, the hard, laminated edges of the bookmark cutting into my palm where I'm gripping it so tightly.

When he continues to stalk toward me, I feel my heart begin to race in my chest, and I break my code of silence.

"Gage, what are you—" I begin, but he cuts me off when he pulls me roughly against his chest, knocking the book and bookmark out of my hands as he smashes his lips against mine.

And, oh my god, it's fire. He's fire and passion all around me, burning me with his heat. I can't even think about how I've lost what page I was on in my book, something that would normally trouble me to no end.

No, all I can do is feel. Feel the strength of his huge arms around me, the solid press of his massive chest against me, the burning rod of hard steel between his legs pressing against my stomach through his pants.

His hot, wet tongue, stroking into my mouth, staking a claim on not just my body but my soul.

Jesus, he's going to destroy me with this kiss.

His hards are skimming roughly up my thighs until they settle on my ass and he yanks me against him, pressing his straining erection against my suddenly throbbing core.

Just when I feel like I'm going to pass out from lack of breath, he pulls back just enough to allow me to breathe.

I gasp in huge gulps of air as his lips speak against mine, breathing the same air I'm breathing. I feel the wet, feathery slide of them against my swollen flesh as he snarls at me viciously, almost angrily.

"Lie to me! Lie to me and tell me you don't want this, that your pussy isn't weeping for it, and I'll stop."

I try to form the words. God knows I try...but I

can't. I can't fucking do it because he's right. I feel an embarrassing wetness trickling down the insides of my thighs, soaking through my white cheeky panties.

Those blue eyes of his are piercing me knowingly, holding me captive better than any locks or chains ever could. They darken when I don't speak, and I feel his hand slip between my legs.

"Christ," he chokes out, his pupils dilating and his nostrils flaring, "That fucking thing is soaked, baby."

Something warm unfurls within me at the way he calls me "baby," and I can't help the whimper that escapes me.

"I know, sweetheart," he soothes me in response to my whimper, his lips skimming over my neck, dropping wet kisses all along the column. I can't stop my head from falling back to allow him better access anymore than I can stop the sun from rising.

"That little pussy aches, doesn't it?" he says sympathetically as he kisses the rise of my breast that's exposed at the top of the little floral dress. "I'm going to make it all better."

The next thing I know his hands are pulling my dress up over my head, leaving me standing before him in nothing but my soaking wet panties.

Before I have a chance to raise my hands up to

cover my exposed breasts, he leans down and takes one in his mouth, sucking greedily on it.

I groan as a zap of electricity shoots from where he's worrying my nipple between his teeth straight down to my swollen sex.

"Gage," I whine his name, not sure what I'm wanting. Do I want him to stop? No. Do I want him to keep going? No, but, yes. Fuck, I don't know. I can't think. My mind is frazzled. I'm nothing but a bundle of nerves and sensations, hyper sensitized to the feeling of his tongue worshipping me while his hands rove over my stomach to slip into the top of my panties as he tugs them down.

"I need another hit," he rasps against my skin. "Need another taste of that juicy little pussy. Been driving me wild thinking about it every night, remembering the sweet taste of it on my tongue as I fuck my fist, wasting this cum that's meant for you."

"Oh, god," I groan out when he drops to his knees and licks me from slit to clit, both his tongue and his words scandalizing me in filthy pleasure.

"Don't worry, baby," he tells me in between licks, "we're going to put this cum where it belongs this time, aren't we?"

He latches onto my clit and begins sucking it with

rhythmic pulses of his tongue, and I can't help myself from screaming out, "Ahhh! Yes!"

"Right here in between these sweet virgin thighs," he growls as I hear the sound of his zipper coming down.

The next thing I know I'm being lifted off my feet as Gage stands, his engorged cock sticking out from his pants and pointing straight up at me.

I instinctively wrap my arms around his neck to hold on as he lowers me onto his shaft while simultaneously thrusting upward.

"Look at me," he orders me, and my eyes meet his. His eyes are burning into me with a possessive glint that takes my breath away. "Don't look away, baby. I want to look at you while I make you mine."

I don't realize he's not all the way inside me until I feel a sharp pain as he grunts and pushes upward while pulling me down. I scream as I feel my hymen ripping open, but Gage doesn't stop. "Ah, fuck, baby... so tight," he grits out as he pushes resolutely forward with a harsh curse until he's bottomed out inside me.

I'm clinging to him for dear life, my whole body trembling and my breath coming out in short little pants as the sharp pain begins to reside only to be replaced by a great pressure.

He's still as I whimper, his arms banded tight

around me, every muscle in his body taut. "That little pussy needs to get used to me fast, baby. I'm not going to be able to hold off much longer," he groans against my shoulder.

I wiggle a bit, trying to get more comfortable or ease the pressure, but that only makes him slide within me a bit, poking me harder. His guttural groan seems tortured, and then he's taking charge again, sliding in and out of me. "Fuck, can't stop, baby. Gotta have you," he grunts out as he starts out slowly but then amps up until he's thrusting his hips up into me at a furious pace, bouncing me up and down in his arms like I'm a rag doll that weighs nothing.

With each thrust of his hips, something is spiking deep within me. He's hitting this spot I never even knew existed, and I feel the pressure building, tingling into something that is a mixture of pain and pleasure but hints at the promise of more. I don't know what the hell it is, but I find myself throwing my hips down to meet his upward thrusts, searching for it.

"Oh, fuck yes, baby. Fuck me back," his voice is clipped in between his pants. "Throw that sweet little pussy down on me. My hot, horny, perfect little virgin."

He captures my lips with his, thrusting his tongue into my mouth in tempo with his strokes before nibbling on my lip, and god, he tastes delicious, like pure male and power and sin.

"Look at me, Ava," he commands when he finally stops kissing me long enough to pull back and stare down into my eyes.

My eyes immediately snap open to obey him. His eyes are burning blue flames as he tells me, "This pussy is mine. You're mine. From now on. You understand me?"

I don't know if it's the way he claims me with his words or the way he hits that spot deep inside harder, but suddenly I feel every muscle in my body spasm. My sex pulses violently around him, and those tremors spread out from there to cause my legs to shake uncontrollably too.

"Goddamn, Ava. Falling open all around me, coming on my dick." His breathing becomes harsh. "I'm there too, baby. Oh fuck!" He throws his head back as he continues to hammer into my body that's gone completely lax in his arms, the squelching sounds of my wetness echoing in the room all around us. "Here I come," he announces his own orgasm before he climaxes with a shout and a curse. I feel his seed jetting deep into me in hot splashes. He's like a geyser, releasing spurt after spurt into me until I can feel myself overflowing, his release trickling out of me to drip down over him and onto the floor.

Still seated deep within me, he carries me over to the bed and lays us down on it facing each other.

He kisses my forehead, my cheeks, my jaw, all while petting me all over, stroking my hair.

He's still hard within me, but he makes no move to take me again. Instead, he just gathers me close to his chest and wraps me up in him, holding me like I'm the most precious thing in his world.

I close my eyes and allow myself to take comfort in him for now, memorizing the feel of him inside him, the sensation of his strong arms around me, the way I'm completely wrapped up in him.

Because I know now that I *have* to escape here. This feels too good. *He* feels too good, and I can't fight him anymore. Not after this.

If I don't leave, he'll destroy me. I'll come to crave him until I can't breathe.

He'll devour my soul.

CHAPTER SEVEN

Gage

I FEEL the moment she slips away from me and promptly wake up. I keep my eyes closed, feigning sleep, though, sure that she's just going to slip in and out of the bathroom and return to my arms.

I know I didn't imagine her response to me earlier. Just remembering how her sweet, tight, little pussy spasmed around me makes me painfully hard again.

Fuck, I need to have her again. I wanted her again immediately after that first time, but I forced myself to refrain. I was already rougher than I should have been with her for her first time, but dammit, she has the kind of pussy that a man loses his mind to. I couldn't control myself once I got inside her.

I hadn't planned on taking her that way—certainly not tonight either. But I was full of tension when I came in today. And when she bent over in that pretty little dress, the perfect little globes of her ass just peeking out around those tiny goddamned panties, I lost it. Fucking lost the last shred of restraint I've been holding onto. I've been in a perpetual state of blue balls ever since she's been here, no matter how much I jacked off, and tonight, the pressure was just too much.

Ava's piece of shit father thought he could get away with not holding up his end of our bargain. My guys found out he still had yet to shut down his little human trafficking operation, and I can't allow that infraction to go unpunished.

I'm sure my men have taken care of the problem by now, and I've given them the go-ahead to use whatever force necessary to deal with the issue.

If that means that asshole is dead by now, then the world will only be a better place in my opinion. I hate it for Ava, but I sense there will be no love lost between them at this point. She hasn't asked a word about her father since the day he gave her to me, and I can't blame her. I have a feeling he died to her that day, and rightfully so.

A stab of unexpected conscience pricks at me. I accepted her as a bribe—but the difference is I love her and want to keep her. Yes, I love her. I don't know at what point I realized it, but it's true. I'm completely fucking in love with Ava Sinclair—in an obsessive, almost psychotic way. I'll do anything to keep her. Anything to make sure she's safe, and eventually she *will* be happy here with me.

I frown at that thought and realize that Ava still hasn't come back to bed. I get up and go into the sitting room where I accosted her earlier.

Her dress is gone.

I curse and hurriedly pull my pants up before heading for the open door.

I find her at the bottom of the stairs heading for the front door and am hit with a sudden sense of deja vu as I recall how she ran from me the first day I brought her here.

I stop in my tracks as a wave of reality crashes over me like a ton of bricks.

As if she senses me, she turns, her eyes wide as she sees me standing at the top of the staircase looking down at her.

I can see her beginning to tremble from here, and I deflate.

I don't want her fear. I don't want her resentment.

And I finally realize that's all I'll ever have with her if I make her stay here against her will. She'll be my prisoner.

Oh, her body might respond to me, but I'll never have her heart and soul. She'll always keep her true self locked off from me, living a half life, fighting herself day to day, guilt-ridden by her body's response to me when her mind hates me and what I've done.

I really am a monster.

I once thought I'd do whatever it takes to keep her, her wishes be damned. She'll come around in time. But looking down into her soft, doe-colored eyes, I suddenly see how I've been deluding myself.

My little Georgia peach will never be happy in a cage—no matter how gilded it is.

And my god, the rough way I took her. It was her first time. I should have been gentler. Christ's sake, no wonder she's running from me.

She'll never get over me kidnapping her. She'll see me as just the same as her father. Someone who buys and sells humans.

And I can't bear the thought of her thinking of me as that sort of monster.

Heart heavy but mind made up with what I have to do to prove I really love her, I turn my back on her, silently giving her permission to go.

I can't watch her leave me, though. I can't watch the one good thing to ever light my dark world walk out that door.

And when I hear the heavy thud of the door closing, pain like I've never known wracks my entire body until I'm shaking so bad I collapse to my knees, my fists clenched tightly as I reign in the urge to chase after her and drag her back here.

Ava.

———

Ava

He let me go. Part of me is still in disbelief that he simply turned and walked away when he found me fleeing him after our passionate coupling during which he'd announced that I was his from then on. I'd fully expected him to chase me down and chain me to his bed.

I'm thoroughly relieved that he didn't. I need to get away from him. I need my freedom. I can't lose myself in him.

The man who kidnapped me and then let my father trade my freedom away. The man who effectively bought me like I was a possession—whether he chooses to see it that way or not.

Why then do I feel so empty and depressed?

I didn't have anywhere to go after leaving Gage. I couldn't go home to a father who would so callously trade my life for his own. I never wanted to see or hear from him again.

And I felt so irrevocably changed after Gage that I knew I could no longer go home and pretend to be the silly, naive little girl that I was before.

So I took off into the city. By some miracle, I was offered a job and a place to stay at the first diner I walked into. The owner is a kind old woman who took me under her wing. I already regard her as the mother I never had.

I've definitely gone down in the world. No college. Working a simple job, but I have food to eat and a roof over my head, and most of all, I have my freedom.

But I'm not happy, and it's not the lack of material comforts and riches that troubles me.

I just feel...empty. So empty.

It's like I'm perpetually cold after feeling the heat of the sun. Nothing in my life can compare to it.

I'm not disappointed that Gage didn't fight for me. I can't be. Though I am filled with embarrassment and shame at the thought of him. I still remember my body's wanton response to him that night. I'm taunted by dreams of his hands on me and wake up wet and throbbing. I've tried touching myself the way he did, but nothing relieves the ache.

I'm so pathetic I don't even know how to give myself the kind of relief his body gave me.

And then I'm filled with humiliation when I realize that I was just a challenge to him. Once he had me, he let me go.

Just another notch on his belt. That's all I was.

All that possessive talk was just that—talk in the heat of the moment. He obviously didn't mean any of it. And that's good really. I don't want to be his captive forever. Things worked out better than I could have ever hoped.

They did.

And being an inexperienced virgin, there's no way I could satisfy a man like Gage who's probably been with women who knew what they were doing, women who know how to pleasure a man beyond his wildest dreams.

And I'm nothing but a girl. A silly, stupid little girl who went and fell in love with her captor.

The realization comes to me slowly, but I have to recognize it for what it is. Either I have severe Stockholm Syndrome or somewhere along the way I fell in love with my dark, brooding kidnapper.

Or maybe I'm just fuck struck.

Who the hell knows?

All I know is Gage is in my dreams every night. His image flits across my mind all the time. Every time I close my eyes, his blue eyes are there piercing me, calling me *his*. My body still thrums with energy every second of the day like it's just waiting for him, but that's impossible.

He let me go.

I close up the diner and begin the short trek to Miranda's apartment. She's been looking tired lately. The poor woman runs herself ragged going in early every day to open up and staying late to close up the diner. I finally convinced her to let me take over closing up the place so she can go home earlier and get more rest. I'm younger than she is and can handle the longer hours better. Plus, I try to keep myself busy to keep my mind off of Gage and all the confusing feelings he elicits in me.

The city streets are still bustling with pedestrians even at this time of night, people catching late-night shows and dinners. Because of all the foot traffic, I've always felt relatively safe traversing the streets at night for the short walk to where I stay with my boss.

That's why I'm totally caught off guard when I feel a rough hand slap over my mouth as I'm jerked backward into a dark alley.

I instinctively begin to kick and scream against the foul-smelling hand, my panic kicking up into overdrive when I'm pressed face-first against the cold brick of a building, a huge form reeking of body odor and stale alcohol pinning me in place.

"Feisty little thing, aren't you?" a cold voice chuckles in my ear. "That's okay. I like it when they fight."

When he removes his hand from my mouth to begin pushing up my skirt, I scream the only name that comes to mind, my piercing cry echoing in the dark alleyway, "Gage!"

As if he's a demon that I've summoned from the depths of hell with my soul-piercing scream, he's suddenly there, yanking the putrid-smelling man off of me, his fist smashing into his face, blood spraying from the man's now-broken nose, before he flings his unconscious form to the ground.

I don't know if he's killed him or just knocked him out, and I can't find it in me to care because all I can think is *he's here! He saved me. He came for me.*

I sob with relief, and the shock becomes too much. My legs give out from underneath me, but Gage is there, catching me as I fall, cradling me against his big chest, running his hands over me, making sure I'm okay.

"Jesus, Ava. Are you okay, princess?" he asks me as he strokes my hair back from my face.

"You came," I say, still dazed by his sudden appearance.

"Of course I came, baby. I'll always come for you." I notice his hands are shaking as he cups my face. "You didn't really think I'd leave you on these streets all alone, did you?"

I look up to find his blue eyes looking down at me earnestly, and I finally realize...that prickling sensation that's constantly at the back of my neck...it's him. I've felt his presence all along. He's been watching me all this time. He never really did let me go.

Maybe I should be mad about that, but I can't summon any anger. All I feel is relief—especially when I realize what could have just happened to me if he hadn't shown up when he did.

He must mistake my silence for anger, though, because he curses, his jaw hardening, "Goddammit, Ava, I know I let you think I let you go, but I'm not sorry I've been watching you all this time like some fucking stalker. If that makes you hate me even more, then so be it. I know you want nothing to do with me, but I can't just leave you out here unprotected. Do you know how hard it is for me not to snatch you back to me every fucking day that your existence taunts me?"

I look up at him, his hard, beautiful face, my dark angel, and swallow, summoning up all my courage.

"Then do it," I tell him softly, raising my hand to stroke the dark stubble that lines his strong jawline.

His brow furrows as he glares down at me, every muscle in his body rigid where he still holds me cradled in his arms. "What are you playing at, Ava? Now's not the time for your sarcasm. Push me, and I won't be able to stop myself."

I shake my head. "I'm not playing. Kidnap me again."

He continues to stare down at me disbelievingly, and I see the muscles of this throat work as he fights for words.

"I don't hate you, Gage. I..." I stumble over my own words as I try to confess how I really feel to him. "I've missed you."

He's perfectly still for a beat, and then his eyes flare with heat, burning down into me as his arms tighten around me. "Do you know what you're saying, Ava? Don't fucking play with me. If I take you again, there will be no letting you go this time. You'll be mine completely." He shakes his head before continuing,

"And not because I accepted you as payment for a debt. I don't see you as a thing to be traded. I never have, baby. I just want you so badly. I was willing to keep you any way I could."

"But you let me go," I point out, a bit of my insecurity creeping back in.

He must notice it because he laughs jaggedly, "Because I love you, Ava. I fucking love everything about you and I couldn't stand the thought of you being unhappy, feeling trapped with me. I want you. God knows how much I want you, but I don't want to force you."

His eyes bore into mine with new intensity when he delivers his next statement, "That's why I want you to understand. It took every ounce of willpower I had to let you go before. I love you enough to do that once. I don't know if I have the strength to do it again. Hearing you walk out that door, Ava," his voice cracks before coming out roughly, "it about killed me."

My heart is beating a staccato rhythm in my chest. He loves me. He said he loves me. *That's* why he let me go. Not that he was bored with me. Not that he'd conquered me.

And he's been watching over me all this time, like my very own dark guardian angel.

I know I should be freaked out by that, but I'm not.

It reassures me. He loves me enough to let me go and watch over me from afar and make sure I'm okay.

A burst of happiness soars through me, and I feel moisture pricking my eyes.

Gage looks distressed at my tears, but I silence whatever he was going to say by pressing my head into the crook of his neck and murmuring my own truth, "I love you too, Gage."

He pulls back from me before looking down at me sharply. "What did you say?" he asks.

I begin to repeat myself, but all I get out is, "I love —" before his lips crash down onto mine fervently, kissing me with all the pent-up lust and love that swells between us.

"You're never escaping from me again, baby," he warns, his lips brushing against mine.

"Good. I don't want to," I admit, submitting completely to being his willing captive.

Gage. My kidnapper. My protector. My lover.

Seven Years Later

Gage

MY COCK IS rock hard as I watch Ava, my wife, walking across my office to where I sit behind my desk. Yes, I've gone legit. No more managing the underworld of New York. I turned that over to my cousin and went straight after I found out I had an aptitude for investment. Well, I always knew I had a knack for it, but now instead of investing in seedy projects, I invest in ones on the up and up.

I did it all for Ava. Her and our three beautiful

children. Scott, Billy, and little Claire. I didn't want to be gone all hours of the night putting myself in dangerous situations when I have such a perfect family waiting at home for me. And I wanted to do something my kids could be proud of. Their daddy is a legitimate businessman. They won't have to hedge to their friends about what I do like I'm in the mob or something.

And my woman. God, my woman. She's everything. The air I breathe. The reason I wake up in the morning.

She found her calling as well. Turns out she's great at teaching, so she's an online professor. She has a love for learning and is a lifelong student, always furthering her education and taking new classes that interest her whether they go toward earning another degree or not. She's read nearly all the books I've never had the time to read in our library and is always adding more to the collection.

Though she's not really my captive anymore and can go anywhere she pleases, I was greatly relieved when she chose to set up an office next door to mine and work at home.

I don't think I could have taken all those young college guys drooling all over her. This way she's here with me all the time where I know she's safe and

where we can get our fix on each other when needed—
like right now.

Scott and Billy are still at school and Miranda, the
lady who took Ava in when she left me, is watching
Claire. Ava had grown so attached to the woman that
when she moved back in here with me, I'd hired the
woman on so she could be close to Ava, who needs her
as a mother figure in her life.

I have to say the woman's grown on me as well, and
the kids adore her and her cooking. Of course, they like
Jose and Rosa too, both of whom spoil them and who
are actually pretty good friends with Ava too now that
she's gotten past their part in her earlier captivity. She
realizes now they were only doing what I told them to.

As far as Ava's father goes, she's only spoken of
him to me once since the day he essentially sold her to
me, and that was to say that she no longer hated him
but that she never wanted to waste another thought on
him ever again. When I found out he'd been killed by
another prominent figure of the underworld, I spared
her the news. She wouldn't want to hear it anyway.

"What can I do for you, Mrs. Morelli?" I ask her as
she finally reaches me, stepping between my spread
legs as I place my hands on her shapely little hips. She
still wears those pretty little floral dresses that taunt
me by brushing against her thighs.

"I just came to see if you needed help releasing any pressure, Mr. Morelli," she tells me saucily, her fingers tracing over the exposed ink on my arms where my sleeves are rolled up. She loves to trace the lines of my tattoos, and I've gotten more just so she'll be enticed to touch me more.

"As a matter of fact, I do," I tell her huskily, as I begin lifting up her dress only to find that she's not wearing any panties.

"Goddamn it, Ava," I growl I as I see the moisture glistening on the front of her clit.

"Yes?" she cocks her head at me innocently while my cock begins to weep at the sight of her tight little snatch.

"You're telling me you've been walking around here all day with this sweet little peach uncovered just begging to be eaten?"

I don't give her a chance to answer before I'm tasting her. Her fingers dig into my hair as I immediately start tongue fucking her, lapping up all her sweet peaches and cream taste. She's moaning and whimpering, music to my ears.

I continue to eat her out until her legs are shaking and she's begging me, making nonsensical noises, and I can't take any more.

My cocks needs to be inside her. *Now.*

She whimpers when I pull my mouth from her, but I'm quick to reassure her. "There, there. I'll make it all better soon, baby."

"Hurry," she moans as I quickly unsheathe myself and pull her down onto my lap, lowering her onto my eager cock that's sticking straight up from my pants. Fuck, I love when she gets so hot she's impatient like this.

"Gage," she pants my name as I stretch her out and then bottom out within her.

"Fuck, yes, baby," I breath against her neck before kissing her lips in hot, wet kisses. Her tongue strokes wildly against mine, kissing me back, making my cock swell within her. Fuck, she keeps this up I won't last three pumps.

"Ride me, baby," I grit out, giving her this freedom, knowing how much she likes to take charge sometimes and set the pace.

My shaft is tingling with electricity with each slide of her wet hole against me. Fuck, she's dripping, her juices sliding down to coat my balls that are so tight I'm fixing to blow any minute.

My jaw is tight and my breathing is labored as I work to keep from coming. I need her to get hers first. Keeping this perfect woman who I'm lucky enough to call mine satisfied is my number one purpose in life.

But damn, when she rides me like this, her full tits bouncing prettily in my face, it's all I can do to keep from shooting.

I feel the telltale churning in my balls and know it won't be long now, so I reach between us and begin rubbing her swollen clit in circles.

I feel the first ripples of her orgasm, and she throws her head back, her entire body flushed with pleasure. She's never been more fucking beautiful than when she's in the throes of passion like this. I feel my own heartbeat tick up at the sight.

"Yes, baby, just like that. Come for me. Come on your man's dick," I order her, pressing on her clit harder, and she explodes.

I feel the moment her orgasm rips through her, her pussy clenching and spasming around me, sucking my own release up out of my tight balls. I can't hold back any longer and thrust up into her while my seed gushes from me to pump up into her, splashing her womb as I claim her in a way no one else ever will.

She collapses against me and lets me hold her. I stroke her hair in our afterglow, thanking God for the millionth time that she's mine.

"You're never getting away from me, baby," I whisper into her ear while still petting her.

"Good. I don't want to," she whispers into my

neck, my precious girl, gifting me with her love time and again, bathing me in her light and goodness.

Changing me for the better.

She might have started off my captive, but I'm *her* prisoner now. She owns me heart, mind, body and soul.

My Ava. My little Georgia peach.

THE END

More from Emma Bray

Connect with Emma!

Visit Emma's website to get a FREE book you can't get anywhere else: www.authoremmabray.com.